Tools Search Notes Discuss Go!

CONTINENTS OF THE WORLD

Discovering Asia's Land, People, and Wildlife

A MyReportLinks.com Book

David Aretha

MyReportLinks.com Books
an imprint of

Enslow Publishers, Inc.

Box 398, 40 Industrial Road
Berkeley Heights, NJ 07922
USA

MyReportLinks.com Books, an imprint of Enslow Publishers, Inc. MyReportLinks®
is a registered trademark of Enslow Publishers, Inc.

Library of Congress Cataloging-in-Publication Data

Aretha, David.
Discovering Asia's land, people, and wildlife / David Aretha.
v. cm. — (Continents of the world)
Includes bibliographical references and index.
Contents: Asia world's largest continent — Land and climate — Animal and plant life — People and culture — Economy — History.
ISBN 0-7660-5183-8
1. Asia—Juvenile literature. [1. Asia.] I. Title. II. Series.
DS5.A73 2004
950—dc22
2003016487

Printed in the United States of America
10 9 8 7 6 5 4 3 2 1

To Our Readers:
Through the purchase of this book, you and your library gain access to the Report Links that specifically back up this book.
The Publisher will provide access to the Report Links that back up this book and will keep these Report Links up to date on **www.myreportlinks.com** for three years from the book's first publication date.
We have done our best to make sure all Internet addresses in this book were active and appropriate when we went to press. However, the author and the Publisher have no control over, and assume no liability for, the material available on those Internet sites or on other Web sites they may link to.
The usage of the MyReportLinks.com Books Web site is subject to the terms and conditions stated on the Usage Policy Statement on **www.myreportlinks.com**.
A password may be required to access the Report Links that back up this book. The password is found on the bottom of page 4 of this book.
Any comments or suggestions can be sent by e-mail to comments@myreportlinks.com or to the address on the back cover.

Photo Credits: AP/ Wide World Photos, p. 31; Artville, p. 1; © 2000–03 The Metropolitan Museum of Art, p. 30; © Corel Corporation, pp. 3, 13, 18, 20, 24, 26, 28, 32, 35, 36, 41, 43, 44; GeoAtlas, p. 10; Marijke J. Klokke, p. 42; MyReportLinks.com Books, p. 4; PBS/© 2000 WGBH, pp. 14, 16; Photos.com, p. 23; Smithsonian National Zoological Park, p. 22; Takashi Toyooka, p. 39.

Cover Photo: Artville (map); © Corel Corporation; Photos.com.

Contents

MyReportLinks.com Books

Great Books, Great Links, Great for Research!

The Report Links listed on the following four pages can save you hours of research time by **instantly** bringing you to the best Web sites relating to your report topic.

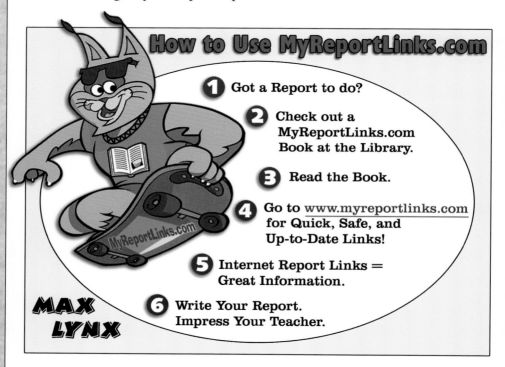

How to Use MyReportLinks.com

1. Got a Report to do?
2. Check out a MyReportLinks.com Book at the Library.
3. Read the Book.
4. Go to www.myreportlinks.com for Quick, Safe, and Up-to-Date Links!
5. Internet Report Links = Great Information.
6. Write Your Report. Impress Your Teacher.

MyReportLinks.com

MAX LYNX

The pre-evaluated Web sites are your links to source documents, photographs, illustrations, and maps. They also provide links to dozens—even hundreds—of Web sites about your report subject.

MyReportLinks.com Books and the MyReportLinks.com Web site save you time and make report writing easier than ever!

Please see "To Our Readers" on the copyright page for important information about this book, the MyReportLinks.com Web site, and the Report Links that back up this book. Please enter **CAS1684** if asked for a password.

Report Links

The Internet sites described below can be accessed at http://www.myreportlinks.com

*EDITOR'S CHOICE

▶InterKnowledge—Asia
Site includes information on India, Indonesia, Malaysia, Myanmar, Nepal, Pakistan, Papua New Guinea, Russia, Thailand, and Vietnam.

*EDITOR'S CHOICE

▶The World Factbook
The World Factbook Web site provides profiles of countries in Asia and around the world. Each profile provides vital information about the country, including geography, government, people, economy, and other related information.

*EDITOR'S CHOICE

▶Perry-Castañeda Library Map Collection: Asia Maps
On this site you can view maps of countries in Asia, as well as historical maps of the region.

*EDITOR'S CHOICE

▶The Smithsonian National Zoo: Asia Trail
Take a tour of the Asia Trail, an exhibit where you will see photos of Asian elephants, sloth bears, giant pandas, clouded leopards, and many more animals of Asia.

*EDITOR'S CHOICE

▶Everest
This site from PBS provides information about Mount Everest, located in Nepal, and a look at the people who have tried to climb it.

*EDITOR'S CHOICE

▶Endangered Species: Panda Facts
On this site from the World Wildlife Fund you can read about the giant panda, an endangered species found only in China.

Report Links

The Internet sites described below can be accessed at http://www.myreportlinks.com

▶Building Big: Petronas Towers
Read about the Petronas Towers, located in Malaysia. These towers are the tallest in the world, reaching 1,483 feet.

▶Bureau of East Asian and Pacific Affairs: Country Information
From the Bureau of East Asian and Pacific Affairs you will learn about the countries located in that region, including China, Mongolia, and Vietnam.

▶Bureau of European and Eurasian Affairs: Country Information
From the Bureau of European and Eurasian Affairs, you can find information on the countries located in central Asia. Russia, Kazakhstan, Uzbekistan, and others are included.

▶Bureau of Near Eastern Affairs: Country Information
From the U.S. State Department's Bureau of Near Eastern Affairs you will find information on Iraq, Saudi Arabia, Syria, and the other countries in that region.

▶Bureau of South Asian Affairs: Country Information
On this site from the Bureau of South Asian Affairs you can find information on countries located in this region, including India, Afghanistan, and Nepal.

▶Castles of Japan
Learn the history of castles in Japan at this Web site. Search by name or location. Data is included with each image.

▶Demton Khang—The Tibet Museum
Demton Khang was created to memorialize Tibetans who died as a result of Chinese occupation. An online photo gallery is available.

▶The Dragons of Komodo
Learn about the Komodo dragon, including its classification, habitat, physical characteristics, life span, and diet. This site features photos, FAQ's, and information on conservation of the world's largest lizard.

Report Links

The Internet sites described below can be accessed at http://www.myreportlinks.com

Embassy of Japan, Washington, D.C.

The FAQ section on the Embassy of Japan Web site includes information on such topics as business, culture, traditions, holidays, history, food, society, and relations with the United States.

Great Wall of China

On this site you can learn about the construction of the Great Wall of China, the history of the Wall, and more.

History of Russia

This site provides a look at the history of Russia from ancient times to the fall of the Soviet Union.

Iraq—A Country Study

From their Federal Research Division, the Library of Congress presents a study of Iraq. Information includes history, geography, society, economy, national security, and more.

Korean History Project

This organization introduces you to East Asian history through a collection of essays, a time line, and facts and figures.

Manas: India and Its Neighbors

Explore India's culture, landscape, religions, history, politics, and more. Also includes biographies on such notables as Mohandas and Indira Gandhi. Photos are included.

Metropolitan Museum of Art: Time line of Art History

This art history time line includes art from East Asia, Central and North Asia, South and Southeast Asia, and West Asia. Time line includes paintings, hanging scrolls, pottery, and more.

Mohandas Gandhi

On this site from *Time* magazine, you can read a biography of Mohandas Gandhi. With his philosophy of non-violence, he helped India win its independence from Great Britain.

The Internet sites described below can be accessed at http://www.myreportlinks.com

National Heritage Board of Singapore

The National Heritage Board of Singapore presents a virtual tour of its museum. By looking through the present, past, and permanent exhibits, you can view artifacts and learn the history behind them.

National Museum of Japanese History

Learn about natural disasters of Japan, and view a history time line and other exhibits at this Web site. Photos, artwork, maps, and tables are included.

Our Earth as Art: Images of Asia & the Middle East

View these satellite images of Asia and the Middle East. A clickable map also allows you to view other areas of the world. Each image is annotated with information.

Profiles of the World's Great Rivers

View photos, and learn about the world's great rivers. Included is information on China's Yangzte, the longest river in Asia and the third longest in the world.

Southeast Asian Monuments: A Selection of One Hundred Slides

Provided by the Oriental Department of Leiden University of the Netherlands, this site presents a collection of photos of monuments in mainland Southeast Asia. Comments are included.

Soviet Archives Exhibit

The Library of Congress presents this online guided tour of the Soviet Exhibit. Included is the "Internal Workings of the Soviet Union" and "The Soviet Union and the United States."

United Arab Emirates Official Homepage

Take a virtual tour of the United Arab Emirates. This site offers information on government, business, travel, culture, history, nature, geography, the arts, and more.

Vietnam: Journeys of Body, Mind, and Spirit

Take this online journey through Vietnam's history as it explains about the nation's people, culture, geography, economy, and religions. Many photos are included.

Asia Facts

Area*

17,212,000 square miles (44,578,900 square kilometers)

Population‡

3.7 billion

Five Most Populous Countries

- China 1,284,303,705
- India 1,045,845,226
- Indonesia 232,073,071
- Pakistan 147,663,429
- Bangladesh 133,376,684

Highest Point of Elevation

Mount Everest 29,035 feet (8,850 meters)

Lowest Point

Dead Sea −1,349 feet (−411 meters)

Major Mountain Ranges

Himalayas, Karakoram, Kunlun Shan

Major Lakes and Rivers

Caspian Sea, Lake Aral, Lake Baikal, Mekong River, Yangtze River, Kiang River

Major Religions

Hinduism, Islam, Chinese Traditional, Buddhism, Christianity, Judaism

Countries

Afghanistan, Armenia, Azerbaijan, Bahrain, Bangladesh, Bhutan, Brunei, Cambodia, China, Cyprus, East Timor, Georgia, India, Indonesia, Iran, Iraq, Israel, Japan, Jordan, Kazakhstan, Kuwait, Kyrgyzstan, Laos, Lebanon, Malaysia, Maldives, Mongolia, Myanmar, Nepal, North Korea, Oman, Pakistan, Philippines, Qatar, Russia, Saudi Arabia, Singapore, South Korea, Sri Lanka, Syria, Taiwan, Tajikistan, Thailand, Turkey, Turkmenistan, United Arab Emirates, Uzbekistan, Vietnam, Yemen

* *All metric and Celsius measurements in this book are estimates.*
‡ *Population figures were taken from* Time Almanac *2003.*

Chapter 1

World's Largest Continent

It is hard to miss Asia on a world map. The continent covers up almost one third of the earth's landmass, covering about 17 million square miles (44 million square kilometers). Asia is bigger than South America and North America combined. As for population, more people live in Asia than the six other continents combined.

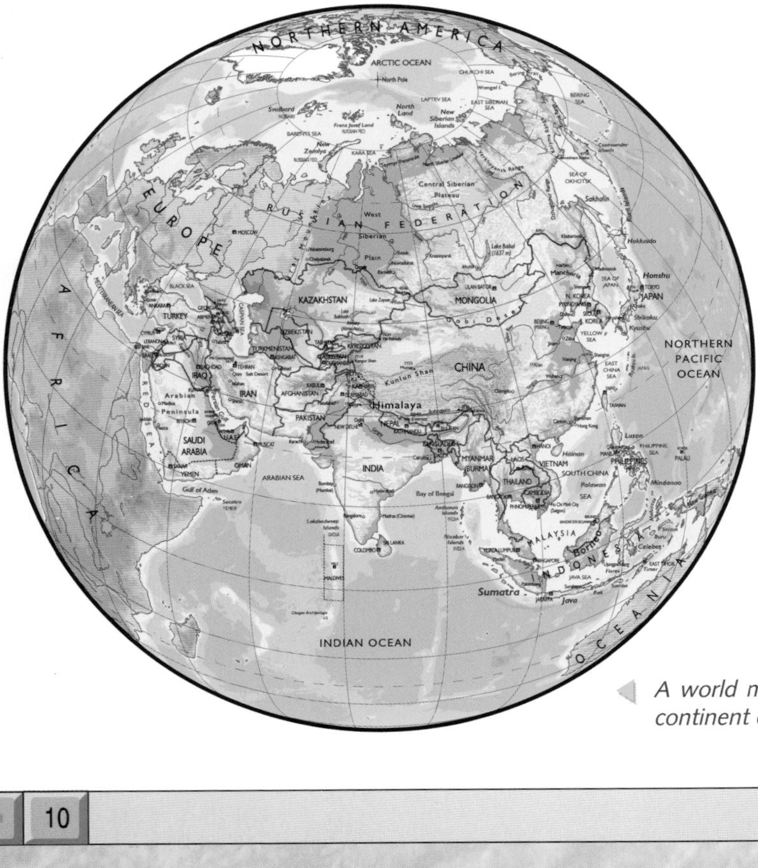

A world map of the continent of Asia.

Broad Boundaries, Billions of People

Many find it surprising how close Asia is to the United States. Only a fifty-one-mile stretch, known as the Bering Strait, separates Asia from Alaska. Indeed, Asia's reach is enormous. The islands of Southeast Asia reach almost to Australia, while in the northwest the Ural Mountains separate Asia from Europe. Asia's western border also touches Africa, where the Sinai Peninsula meets Egypt. People once could walk from Asia to Africa without getting their feet wet.

Of the 6.2 billion people in the world, 3.7 billion live in Asia. About 1.28 billion people reside in China, while 1.05 billion inhabit India. For perspective, consider this: The United States is the world's third most populated country, with just 287 million people.[1]

Regionally Speaking

Breaking the map of Asia up into regions is perhaps the easiest way to study the geography of this vast land. Asia is generally viewed as a group of six regions, each with its own distinctive characteristics.

Southwest Asia includes the Arabian Peninsula and surrounding countries, which are often referred to as a portion of the "Middle East." Many countries comprise this region: Cyprus, Jordan, Israel, Lebanon, Saudi Arabia, Syria, Turkey, Armenia, Azerbaijan, Georgia, Bahrain, Iran, Iraq, Kuwait, Qatar, Yemen, Oman, and the United Arab Emirates. A very small portion of Egypt lies in Southwest Asia as well.

Just to the east of Southwest Asia is South Asia. It is sometimes called the Indian Subcontinent because much of it extends into the Indian Ocean. India falls into this region, of course, as do Pakistan, Nepal, Bhutan, Bangladesh, Sri Lanka, and Maldives.

Southeast Asia is made up largely of island nations. The region includes the countries of Myanmar (Burma), Thailand, Malaysia, Laos, Vietnam, Cambodia, Indonesia, Brunei, East Timor, Singapore, and the Philippines.

The country of China takes up most of East Asia's landmass, which is sometimes referred to as the "Far East." Also in this region are Japan, North Korea, South Korea, Taiwan, and Mongolia.

Russian Asia is just that—the large nation of Russia. It includes the sparsely populated region of Siberia to the north. Temperatures there differ vastly from those in Asia's other regions. A good portion of Russia also lies in Europe.

Finally, Central Asia is made up of six countries ending in "stan"—Kazakhstan, Uzbekistan, Turkmenistan, Kyrgyzstan, Tajikistan, and Afghanistan. These nations sit mainly inland, to the east of Iran and west of China.

Asia's Influence on the World

People in the Western world often struggle to understand the customs of the East. One reason is that the European-based Romance languages—such as English, French, and Spanish—are much different from Asian languages. Also, while the Western world is mostly Christian, most Asians follow different religions.

Over time, Asian cultures have had a great influence on peoples in other parts of the world. As author George B. Cressey wrote: "Asia is not just the biggest and most continental or highest or wettest or most diverse of continents. It is interesting because it is the most human."[2]

Civilization in Asia sprang up in the Middle East's Fertile Crescent more than ten thousand years ago. In addition, all of the world's major religions have roots in Asia, including Christianity, Islam, Judaism, Hinduism,

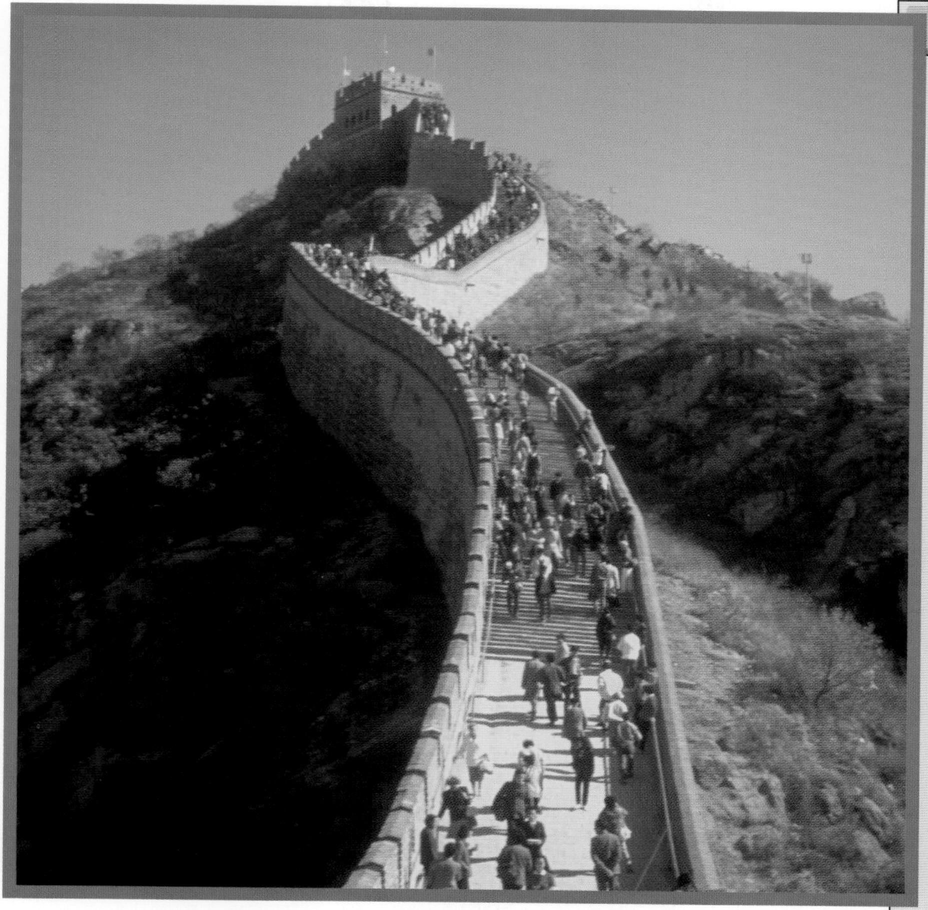

The Great Wall of China is the longest structure ever made. Most of it was built in the late 1400s.

and Buddhism. Biblical figures, including Abraham, Moses, and Jesus, lived in the Middle East. Muhammad and Buddha also were born in Asia.

The people of the ancient Middle East were the first to study medicine, mathematics, and the stars (astronomy). They created written language from picture drawings

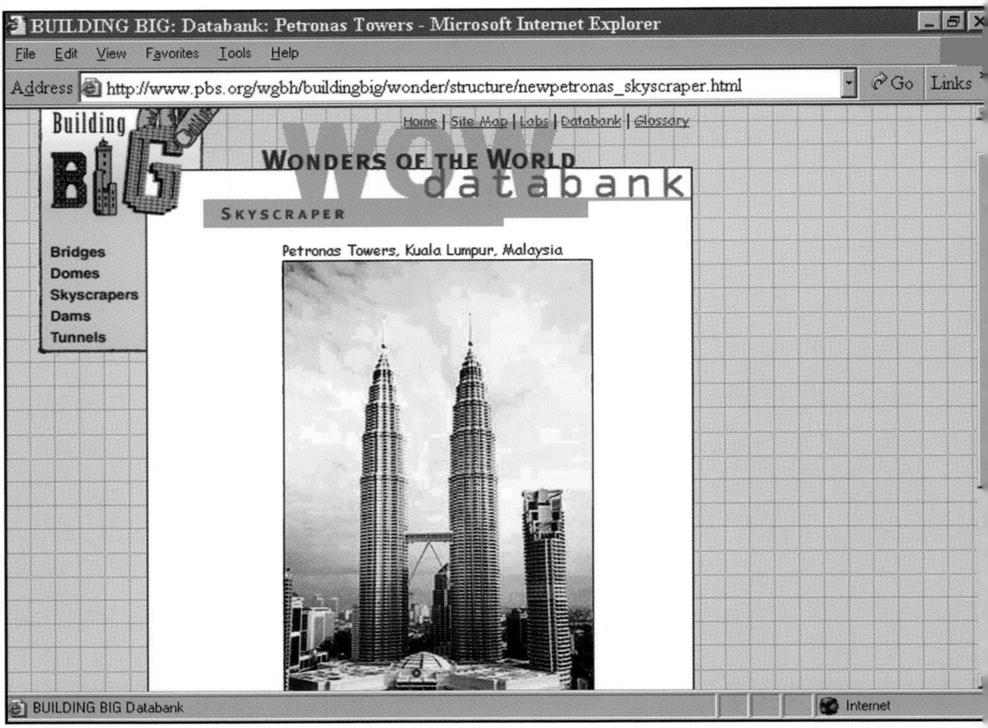

BUILDING BIG: Databank: Petronas Towers - Microsoft Internet Explorer

File Edit View Favorites Tools Help

Address http://www.pbs.org/wgbh/buildingbig/wonder/structure/newpetronas_skyscraper.html Go Links

Building BIG

Home | Site Map | Labs | Databank | Glossary

WONDERS OF THE WORLD databank

SKYSCRAPER

Bridges
Domes
Skyscrapers
Dams
Tunnels

Petronas Towers, Kuala Lumpur, Malaysia

BUILDING BIG Databank

Internet

The Petronas Towers, located in Kuala Lumpur, Malaysia, is the world's tallest building.

(hieroglyphics and cuneiform). They also established the twenty-four-hour day, and they even invented the wheel. People of the Far East created tea, paper, and gunpowder. They also pioneered the study of engineering and used acupuncture to treat ailments.

Many of the world's greatest landmarks—natural and man-made—are in Asia. China boasts the Great Wall, while India has the Taj Mahal. Malaysians created the world's tallest building, the Petronas Towers. Japan, though, is home to the world's most populated metropolis, Tokyo. Indeed, the wonders of Asia go on and on.

Land and Climate

In Asia, the diversity of geology and climate is extraordinary. A person could stand one thousand feet below sea level at one spot, five miles above at another. Incredibly enough, temperature readings in Asia have varied by as much as 219°F (104°C).

Geology

In the north, Asia reaches almost to the polar desert. These lowlands are basically uninhabitable for much of the year. The Siberian forests are beautiful in the summer months, but few take in the view. The Russian people prefer the more mild southern areas of their country, which can still be brutally cold during the winter.

Similar conditions can exist in the highlands of Central Asia, but for different reasons. There, it is the altitude that brings the cold. The most famous mountain in the world—and the tallest—is Mount Everest. It is located on the border of Nepal and Tibet. It towers 29,035 feet (8,850 meters) above sea level. Mount Everest, whose summit was first reached by Sir Edmund Hillary and Tenzing Norgay in 1953, towers over the rest of the Himalayas.

Of the ten highest mountain peaks on the globe, nine are in the Himalayas. The continent's other ranges include the Altai, Elburz, Hindu Kush, Karakoram, Kunlun Shan, Qilian Shan, Qin Ling, Stanovoi, Tian Shan, Yablonovy, and Zagros. The Pamirs, located mainly in Tajikistan, form a central point where many of the other Asian

mountains converge. Raised plateaus in this region bear a resemblance to tabletops. They have been called the "roof of the world."

Just south of the Himalayas is the Indian Subcontinent. It features the Indo-Gangetic Plain, the Thar Desert, and the Deccan Plateau. Its terrain varies greatly, from low, desert-like regions to majestic mountains.

Lowlands prevail to the north and east of the Qilian Shan, Qin Ling, and Nan Ling mountain ranges of China. The Gobi in China is the largest desert in Asia. It could hold the state of California approximately three times over. Its surface, made up largely of small stones, holds very little vegetation.

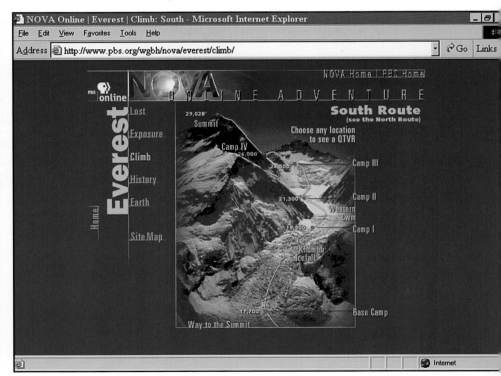

This image shows the south route that most climbers take in their attempt to reach the peak of Mount Everest. Unfortunately, some people that set out to get to the top never make it back.

Features of Land Formations

Asia boasts the sixty-seven tallest mountains in the world. Though majestic, Asia's mountains sometimes create dangerous mudslides. These occur largely because people have cut down trees for heating and building purposes. Once the mountains are barren, heavy rains can turn the terrain to mud and cause catastrophic problems for the people, animals, and vegetation below.

In addition to its cloud-topping mountains, Asia also features several uplands. These smaller mountains and hills cover eastern China, eastern Kazakhstan, parts of Siberia, and such islands as Ceylon and Taiwan. The climate and living conditions are more moderate there than on the taller ranges. This allows cities, towns, and villages to thrive.

Rivers are of vital importance to the people of Asia, since much of the continent is dry. Most of Asia's rivers originate in the mountains. In the Himalayas, ice and snow melt and this water flows downward. The water becomes the lifeblood of lush, green strips below, then winds toward the ocean.

In Southeast Asia, the Mekong River flows some 2,500 miles (4,023 kilometers) from China to Vietnam. It runs past Laos, Thailand, and Cambodia along the way. It is a heavily trafficked river in a densely populated region. In fact, some families live in floating houses on its waters. They raise fish in cages underneath their homes until the fish are large enough to eat or sell.

In northern China and Mongolia, the water level is actually higher than the land. Thus, for four thousand years the Chinese have tried to control its might with dikes. Flood damage has been prevented to some extent,

Bathers go for a swim in the Dead Sea. The bottom of the Dead Sea is the lowest point of the earth. It is also the saltiest body of water on the planet.

though frequent flooding still occurs for those near the water's banks.

The Dead Sea joins Israel and Jordan. It marks the earth's lowest point at −1,349 feet (−411 meters) below sea level. The Dead Sea is the saltiest and most mineral-laden body of water on the planet. The Red Sea separates the Arabian Peninsula from Africa. Brimming with colorful marine life and exotic animals, it provides beautiful contrast to the desert land of Arabia.

In addition to its saltwater seas, Asia features glorious lakes. Lake Baikal in Russia covers 12,162 square miles (31,500 square kilometers) more than a mile long and more than 25 million years old. The salty Caspian Sea, north of Iran, is even larger. At 152,239 square miles (394,297 square kilometers), it has been called the world's largest lake.

Of course, nowhere is water more central to Asian life than on its many islands. The nations of Japan, Taiwan, and the Philippines are islands. So, too, are Indonesia, Brunei, and Sri Lanka. The island of New Guinea, at 316,615 square miles (820,029 square kilometers), is the second largest island on Earth. Borneo ranks third. Many of Asia's islands combine the beauty of the ocean with breathtaking mountain views.

Climate

Asia witnesses the most extreme weather imaginable. The temperature in Verkhoyansk, Russia, once plunged to −90°F (−68°C). Tirat Tsvi, Israel, once experienced a 129°F (54°C) day.

The highs and lows do not begin to tell the entire story. Many of the islands in the southeast are made up of rain forests. Tropical storms there can be dangerous, but they are a better alternative to the unpredictable earthquakes and volcanoes that also accompany life on some of Asia's islands. Indonesia has approximately four hundred volcanoes.

Another hot area is the southern part of the Indian Peninsula. There, residents pay careful attention to monsoons—seasonal wind shifts that mark the beginning of the rainy season. In late June, July, August, and September, it rains almost every day in some parts of India. The rainy season provides good conditions for growing rice and other crops.

Weather in the northern lowlands and central highlands differs drastically. Dry, desert climate prevails in much of Southwestern Asia, from Saudi Arabia and the Persian Gulf region to the large country of Kazakhstan. To the far north, the dry and frigid tundra of Siberia gradually gives way to subarctic conditions.

This woman from the southern region of India is on her way to a festival. The people from this area wear loose clothing because the climate is so hot.

The mountainous regions of Central Asia offer some of the most radically changing weather patterns. Depending on the altitude, one town might be moist enough to sustain rich vegetation while a nearby community receives little rain. Finally, the eastern lowlands offer subtropical conditions. People there experience mild winters, humid summers, and enough rain to sustain the most plentiful rice farming in the world.

Chapter 3 ▶

Animal and Plant Life

A visit to Asia is incomplete without a stop to marvel at the rich wildlife. Animals as diverse as polar bears, camels, pandas, and Komodo dragons all roam the continent. However, many animal habitats are being destroyed at an alarming rate. Asia's rapidly rising population and the killing of animals to sell their body parts have endangered many species.

Wildlife in Different Regions

The type of animals one would encounter in Asia varies drastically from one side of the continent to another. In the northern climes, polar bears, brown bears, arctic foxes, moose, and wolverines endure despite the cold weather. Meanwhile, camels thrive in Saudi Arabia and the continent's other dry, barren regions. Their long legs keep their bodies above the hot sand and their heads above the blowing dust during storms. Their humps can allow survival for many days without water.

The continent's mountains and plateaus are home to such mammals as the yak, lynx, and wolf. In India, jungle mammals enjoy the lush vegetation and moisture. While riding an elephant through one of India's national parks, one might spot a buffalo, a rhinoceros, or even a Bengal tiger. The bamboo forests of China are home to the adorable-looking giant panda. An endangered species, pandas grow to about four feet (1.2 meters) tall and 250 pounds (113.4 kilograms).

The island of Komodo, one of the Indonesian islands, gives its name to the largest of all lizards, the Komodo dragon. These reptiles, another endangered species, are meat eaters and fierce predators. They can grow to lengths of ten feet (3 meters) and weigh up to three hundred pounds (136 kilograms). They can travel at speeds of up to eleven miles per hour (17.7 kilometers per hour). They are can survive both in the water and in trees, and their mouths carry bacteria that can kill people. The king cobra is another deadly reptile. It is found in southern China, Southeast Asia, and India's grasslands. It possesses enough venom to kill an elephant.

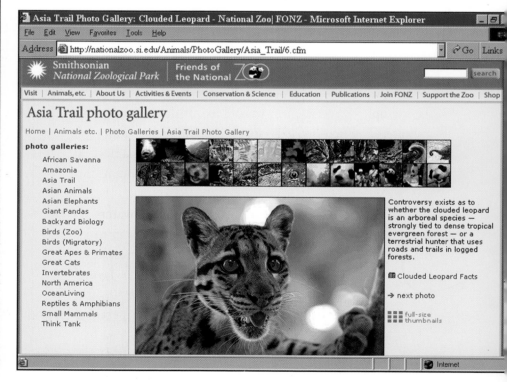

The clouded leopard is one of many interesting animals that are native to Asia.

The Komodo dragon is found on the island of Komodo in Indonesia. These "dragons" are actually reptiles that are known as fierce predators.

The variety of birds in Asia is astounding. The peacock, for example, is native to India and Sri Lanka and does not migrate. The red-headed Japanese crane is a symbol of liveliness and purity in the land for which it is named. It migrates seasonally, but for much of the year it wades in the shallow waters of East Asia.

Finally, fish of all shapes and sizes fill the waters of Asia. Fish are a central part of the traditional diet in most regions of the continent. Bluefin tuna is well known for being made into high quality sushi—mainly in Japan. However, since large-scale fishing began in the 1950s, the bluefin quantity has declined by as much as 95 percent. There are now limits on its catch.

The coral reefs off Indonesia, Malaysia, and the Philippines provide grouper and wrasse, other popular fish for eating. These coral fish are most popular in China

and Hong Kong. Chinese banquets usually include a whole fish either steamed, deep fried, or quick boiled.

Wildlife Preservation

Asia is a continent rich in wildlife, but many of its species fall on the endangered list. There are several reasons for this. Population density is a big problem in some countries, leaving little room for wild animals to roam in their native habitats. Some countries have created national parks and refuges to preserve animal habitats. However, poachers (those who hunt wildlife illegally) remain a problem. Another threat to animal life is the massive leveling of trees. Also, the increasing levels of pollution in Asia's air and water leave animals on the short end of "progress."

As a result, many species are at risk of becoming extinct. Tigers are near the top of the list. The World Wildlife Fund (WWF) estimates that fewer than eight thousand tigers exist in the wild

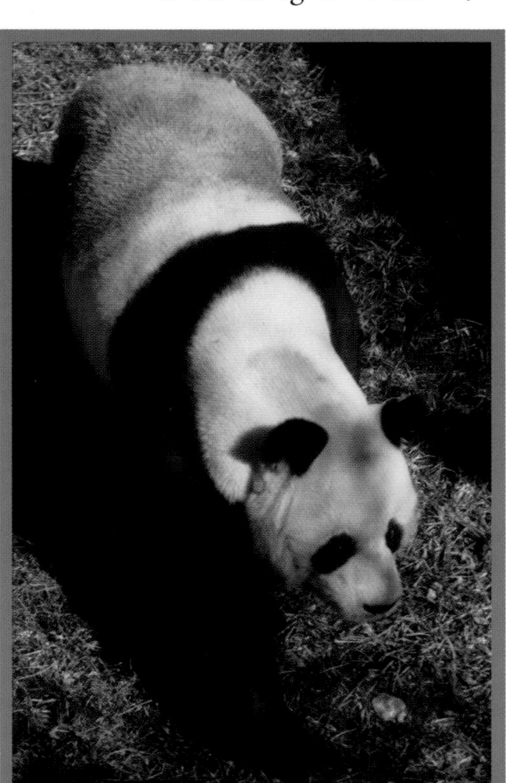

The giant panda is an endangered species native to China. Zoos around the world are trying to add to the panda population through captive breeding programs so that these animals do not disappear.

worldwide.[1] Their skins are highly valued, and many of their body parts have been used in traditional Chinese medicines. Already, several species of tiger have become extinct. That is why in 1998—the Chinese "Year of the Tiger"—several wildlife preservation groups tried to emphasize the importance of cracking down on poachers.

Many wild animals that live in Asia are on the endangered species list. Giant pandas are one of the world's most famous endangered animals. As few as one thousand remain in the wild.[2] No more than fifty thousand Asian elephants exist in the wild.[3] Poachers have long envied their ivory tusks, which are worth a small fortune. The snow leopard, polar bear, and several species of the rhinoceros are also endangered.

Several private groups have been formed to save some of these species, most notably the WWF. Many of these groups campaign for stricter laws against poaching and the illegal sale and trade of endangered animals. Efforts also are being made to protect forests and other animal habitats in Asia. Some groups near India's many national parks have planted native trees around residences for birds and small animals. Saving endangered animals is a big task, but every effort helps.

Plant Life

Asia's diverse climate produces a wide variety of plants. Northern Russia is blanketed in tundra and boreal forest. In other parts of Russia, as well as in China, the climate is more moderate. The regions feature vast scrub and grassland areas.

Asia's many desert regions, particularly in the Southwest, support only vegetation that can survive with little water. Some of the continent's mountainous regions also tend to be

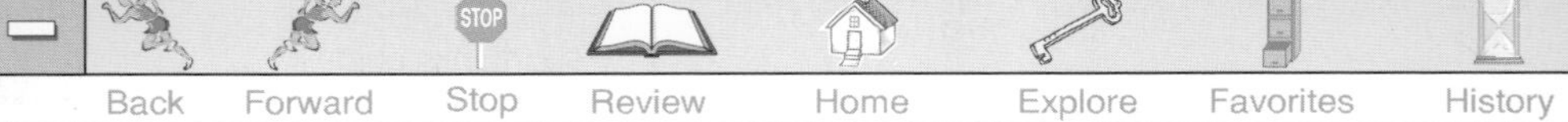

Originally created in Japan, sushi has become a delicacy around the world.

largely barren, though some farming does exist. In the South and Southeast regions of Asia, tropical rainforests and monsoon forests produce plentiful plant life.

Growing and Eating

Not surprisingly, the northern, mountainous, and desert areas of Asia can experience food shortages. Asia's Southern regions traditionally produce plenty of food for consumption and export. However, the rapid growth of population and general economic conditions have caused even fertile Asian lands to experience poverty over the years.

Certain products are plentiful in Asia. China is the world leader in rice production, accounting for roughly 35 percent of the world total. People often use the expression "all the tea in China." That is because China is home to some of the best tea plants on the globe. The Japanese consume and export some of the finest sea produce in the world. Their sushi, rolled fish (many uncooked), has become a delicacy worldwide.

Curry-spiced dishes are popular in India, Thailand, and many other Asian countries. They generally have a stew-like consistency. The classic Vietnamese dish is *pho*—a noodle soup with strong beef stock that includes fresh vegetables. Korea is famous for its *kimchi* (pickled cabbage).

Chapter 4 ▶

People and Culture

Asia not only leads the world in sheer number of people; it also has been the home of many famous people from ancient times. Many of the world's most well-known philosophers and humanitarians were born in various parts of Asia. Moreover, all of the largest world religions began on the continent.

People

A discussion of Asian religious leaders should begin with Abraham. Scholars credit him with fathering three faiths: Judaism, Christianity, and Islam. Biblical scholars disagree about Abraham's exact time frame, but most place him between 1000 and 2000 B.C. According to Genesis, Abraham was born in Ur of the Chaldees, which is now Iraq.

In *Abraham: Journey of Faith*, Tad Szulc wrote: "The outlines of Abraham's life appear first and most fully in Genesis, the first book of the holy scriptures of Judaism and the Christian Bible's Old Testament. Abraham also makes frequent appearances in other Jewish and Christian writings, including the Talmud and the New Testament, and he is mentioned time and again in the Koran, the holy book of Islam."[1]

Another great Jewish and Christian prophet, Moses, is thought to have lived around 1500 B.C. As a young boy, he was found in the Nile River by his adoptive mother. Later, he led the Hebrew people out of captivity in Egypt.

This is an image of the Jerusalem skyline. Located in present-day Israel, Jerusalem is a holy city for people of the Christian, Jewish, and Islamic faiths.

He took them to Mount Sinai, where the Bible says he received God's Ten Commandments.

Christianity traces its roots to the same region. Jesus was born in Bethlehem and raised in Nazareth before his murder in Jerusalem. Accounts of his resurrection from the dead are the basis of the Christian faith. The Asian lands on which Jesus taught are considered sacred by much of the world.

Muhammad, the "Praised One," was born in A.D. 571 and lived in Mecca. He considered Abraham the spiritual ancestor of Islam. Abraham's willingness to sacrifice the life of his son, expressed in the verb *aslama*, is thought to be the basis for the name Islam.

Buddhism is also based in Asia. Buddha Shakyamuni was born as "Siddhartha Gautama" in Lumbini (originally in northern India but now part of Nepal) in 563 B.C. He founded a religion based on meditation, concentration, and enlightenment.

Confucius is Asia's most famous philosopher. Born in China around 551 B.C., Confucius gave out practical advice. He preached that a true gentleman needed to possess five qualities: integrity, righteousness, loyalty, altruism, and goodness. Altruism is a person's willingness to help others. "Do your duty; that is best," he said.[2] For centuries, many Chinese have tried to adhere to his teachings.

India was also home to Mohandas K. Gandhi. With his creed of passive resistance to oppression, Gandhi helped India win its independence from Great Britain in 1947.

Mao Tse-tung was a vastly different kind of Asian leader. He established the Peoples Republic of China in 1949 and was the leader of the Chinese Communist Party for more than forty-one years. He is well known not only for his military skill and his political talent but also for his artistic poems.

Tenzin Gyatso, the fourteenth Dalai Lama of Tibet, lives in exile in India. After Tibet's uprising against Chinese rule in 1959, the Dalai Lama was forced to flee his homeland. Since then, he has won a Nobel Peace Prize for his noble attempts to free Tibet. ". . . [W]ith truth, courage and determination as our weapons, Tibet will be liberated," he said. ". . . [O]ur struggle must remain nonviolent and free of hatred."[3]

Culture

Asian artistic traditions have endured for thousands of years. In fact, Chinese painting is the world's oldest enduring painting tradition. It is characterized by strong brush strokes, often featuring landscapes or flowers. Even writing is art in Asia: Chinese, Arabic, Japanese, and Cambodian calligraphy is both beautiful and functional.

Origami, the folding of paper into shapes, comes from the Japanese words for folding (*ori*) and paper (*kami*). Japan also gave the world the *haiku*, a perfectly balanced poem. A haiku can be about anything; the only rule is in the structure. Haikus are always three lines long. The first and third lines have five syllables, while the second has seven.

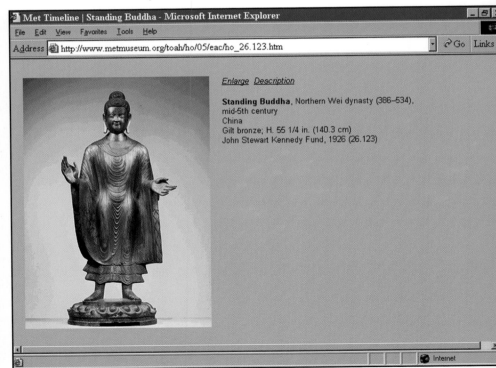

Met Timeline | Standing Buddha - Microsoft Internet Explorer
File Edit View Favorites Tools Help
Address http://www.metmuseum.org/toah/ho/05/eac/ho_26.123.htm
Go Links

Enlarge Description

Standing Buddha, Northern Wei dynasty (386–534), mid-5th century
China
Gilt bronze; H. 55 1/4 in. (140.3 cm)
John Stewart Kennedy Fund, 1926 (26.123)

Internet

Buddhism is one of many religions that can trace its origins to Asia. This sculpture of Buddha was created in China in the A.D. 400s.

Mohandas K. Gandhi (center), also known as the Mahatma, was a religious leader known for his peaceful protests. Time *magazine named him the Person of the Century for the 1900s.*

Care of both body and soul is an important cultural tradition in Asia. Meditation, central to the practice of Buddhism, is the basis of yoga. It is an ancient discipline combining flexibility and introspection. Martial arts, such as Tai Chi and karate, are effective for fighting, but they are really about self-control and discipline. Acupuncture is a Chinese healing method that involves inserting needles into points on the body to encourage the flow of energy. Traditional Asian medicine also uses herbs and potions to promote vitality.

Throughout Asia, the New Year is an important holiday. In China, it is a celebration of renewal. Houses are cleaned, clothes are purchased, and debts are repaid. Fireworks at midnight drive away evil spirits. In Japan, New Year is for spending time with family. At midnight, a gong is struck 108 times, wiping away the 108 sins of the past year. The next morning, people go to the temple to pray for good fortune. In India, Diwali is the Festival of Lights that marks the beginning of the Hindu year.

Each region of Asia has its distinct dress. In China, it is traditional for women to wear the *cheongsam*, or *qipao*. It is a dress with a high neck, closed collar, fitted waist, and side slits. Indian women wear draped dresses made with beautiful textiles called *saris*. Japanese *kimonos* appeared around A.D. 1000. Historically, the ruling Samurai and its armies were identified by the colors of their kimonos and headdresses. Samurai followed a strict code of conduct called *Bushido*.

A karate expert from Okinawa, Japan, puts on a demonstration. Karate's history dates back as early as the 400s B.C.

Chapter 5 ▶

Economy

The Asian economy has fluctuated radically from century to century. Even today, it varies widely from region to region. One constant is that Asians have used their resources to sustain themselves and, in many cases, to thrive.

Historical Economy

The time line of the Asian economy begins thousands of years ago. Evidence indicates that people grew mangoes in Southeast Asia in approximately 5000 B.C. In China, silk making dates back to 3000 B.C. Gunpowder also was invented in China. In these early economies, people bartered, or traded, for goods. The Chinese, about two thousand years ago, invented paper, which eventually led to the manufacture of paper money.

Astronomers hold the Chinese in high regard for their revolutionary creation of seasons. This concept dates to around 100 B.C. The seasons were as important to early Asians as they are today, especially to those who made their living from farming.

Crop farming predates the tenth millennium B.C. in the Middle East. Scientists who have carbon-tested animal remains have dated finds of domesticated sheep to 9000 B.C. Biblical accounts of life along the Sea of Galilee two thousand years ago emphasize the importance of fishing to life in that area. The same can be said for almost every coastal area of Asia in the times before and since.

Industrialization emerged in the 1900s, particularly during World War II and the years immediately following. In *The Asians: Their Heritage and Their Destiny*, Paul Thomas Welty wrote "This was evidenced in Japan, Asia's most industrialized nation, during and after World War II when thousands of city dwellers returned to the country to live with their families, relatives and friends until the crisis was over. But with the coming of a money economy to Asia and the introduction of new Western-oriented ways of life, village self-sufficiency is lessening."[1]

Modern Economy

An economic crisis has taken hold over much of Asia. Of course, the circumstances in each country and region differ. Afghanistan and Iraq, for example, are in the process of rebuilding after war. The national economy in farming countries can depend largely on unpredictable weather.

Chinese workers mine iron and coal and produce garments, textiles, toys, etc. Millions of others farm the land. Japan, which has little farmland, is a world industrial power. Japan relies heavily on the manufacture of cars, ships, computers, and a variety of electronics.

Southwest Asia's most valuable economic resources are oil and natural gas. In fact, the region contains more than half of the world's oil reserves. Saudi Arabia, Iraq, Iran, Kuwait, and surrounding countries obtain large percentages of their national incomes from this industry.

Transportation

China manufactures more than one third of the world's bicycles. Millions, however, are not for export. Many Chinese use the bicycle as their primary form of transportation. In Beijing, cycling roads run alongside virtually every

The Sea of Galilee is located in Israel. It has been an important body of water since biblical times.

major road. Bicycles are also popular in Japan, but in that country rail transportation rules. Tokyo is home to the world's best urban rail transport system. The city's residents are never more than a ten-minute walk from a train station.

No such comforts exist in the desert. Thousands of years ago, frankincense (a type of resin) traders trained camels to make the long journey from southern Arabia to the northern regions of the Middle East. Today, camels can move along desert routes that motorized vehicles are unable to travel.

Tourism

Due to the SARS epidemic in China and other Asian countries in 2003, the tourism industry was hit hard. Thousands of the continent's cities and towns rely on tourism for much of their revenue.

Westerners may feel most at home in Hong Kong, China. Governed by the British until 1997, Hong Kong maintains ancient Chinese traditions while serving as a

The Kowloon skyline at night. Kowloon Island is located just north of Hong Kong. It is known for its shopping areas.

center for international business. One can ride an authentic Chinese junk boat down a river lined with skyscrapers. Tokyo also has a Western influence. Visitors enjoy baseball games, Tokyo Disneyland, and the Hard Rock Cafe as well as sushi bars and sumo wrestling.

Bangkok, Thailand, is one of the world's most vibrant cities. In addition to traditional culture and magnificent temples, visitors find exciting nightlife and glorious beaches. Indeed, much of Southeast Asia has tropical weather, long coastlines, and numerous islands.

Asia also features some of the great wonders of the world. The famed Great Wall of China, built more than two thousand years ago, can be seen from space by astronauts orbiting Earth. Stretching 4,500 miles long, it attracts millions of visitors each year. In the 1600s, the emperor of India, Shāh Jāhan, ordered the construction of a grand palace in memory of his late wife, Agra. It took twenty thousand people to build his Taj Mahal, which remains the most famous symbol of India.

History

Many countries in the world claim to be the "cradle of civilization," meaning those countries believe that human life had started there. Most of these countries are in Asia, including Turkey, India, Iraq, and Armenia. Although we may never know the truth, one thing is for sure; Civilizations in many parts of Asia date back thousands of years.

Ancient Civilizations

The Fertile Crescent, in the area now known as the Middle East, gave birth to many of the earliest civilizations. One of which was Sumer, the rich land between the Tigris and Euphrates rivers. The Sumerians arrived in approximately 4000 B.C. and soon dominated the region. Eventually, the Sumerians were brought under the political control of the Akkadians, who came form nearby Babylonia.

The Babylonian King Hammurabi is known for his Code of Hammurabi. This was a legal system based on the premise that a punishment should match the crime—an eye for an eye. Ultimately, the Babylonians were conquered by the Assyrians. Meanwhile, small groups of Indo-European people moved into what is now Iran near the end of the second millennium B.C. One of these Indo-European peoples, the Persians, would establish a vast empire that would persist for many centuries.

Moving east, the Indus River civilizations flourished in what is now India. By about 2700 B.C., city-states complete with public-works infrastructures were in place.

In China, the first prehistoric dynasty was the Xia, which ruled from about 2000 to 1500 B.C. Japan's prehistory was known as the Jomon period. These ancient Japanese were hunter-gatherers who lived communally. Their settlements grew following the introduction of rice cultivation around 500 B.C.

The Silk Road

The importance of the Silk Road in Asian history is monumental. The Silk Road was actually not one road but a network of routes. By the third century B.C., this had become a center where Persian, Indian, and Greek ideas met. Other routes developed, linking other empires and cultures.

The Silk Road was also used to trade gold, ivory, precious stones, exotic animals, glass, furs, ceramics, jade, bronze, and iron. The most important thing to travel along the Silk Road was religion. The Silk Road was a way for people of different religions to talk to one another and spread there own faith. Buddhism came to China from India along the northern branch of the Silk Road. Christianity traveled along the Silk Road with an early sect that had been driven out of Europe.

The demise of the Silk Road was inevitable by the thirteenth century, in part due to the development of easier and safer trade routes by sea. The shifting sands of the desert buried the old towns and sites along the road.

The Great Dynasties

Genghis Khan was a great warrior who lived in Mongolia in the twelfth and thirteenth centuries. The struggles he faced throughout his life shaped Genghis into a fierce fighter. He conquered and unified much of China and

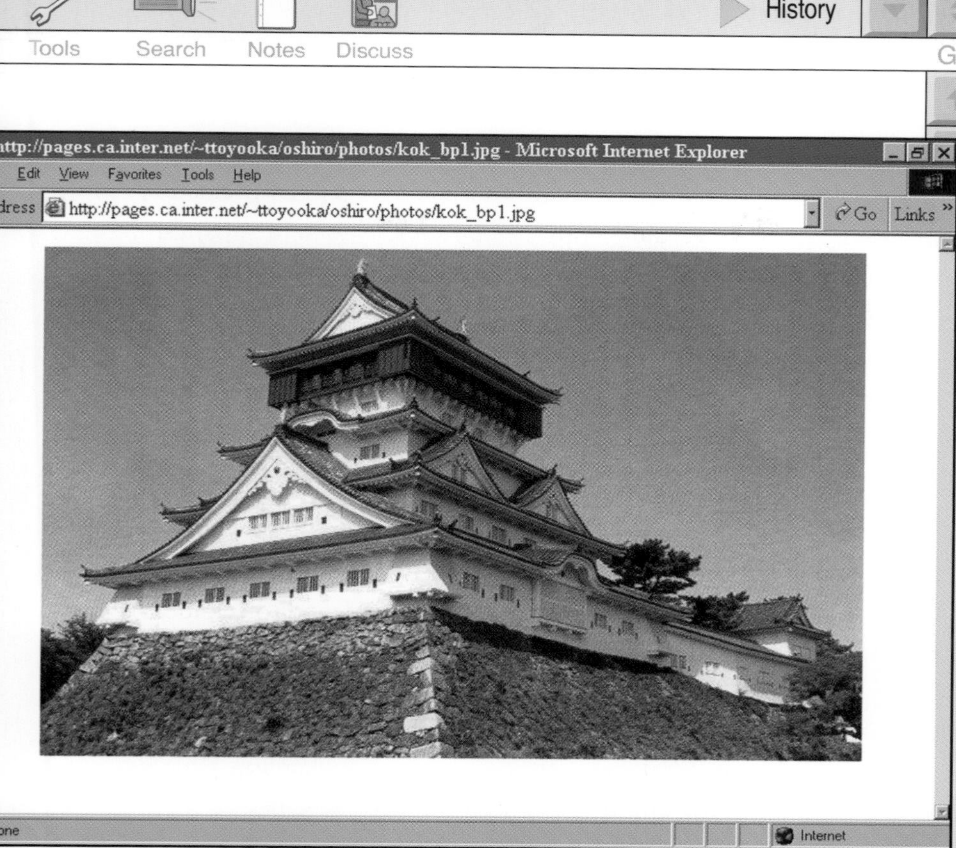

The Kokura-Jo castle is located in the city of Kitykyushu, Japan. Castles such as this one are prime tourist attractions.

Mongolia from a collection of warring tribes into the largest empire on Earth.

Thousands of years of Chinese history can be divided into a few significant dynasties. The Tang Dynasty (618–907) was one of these. The Tang was a time of territorial expansion, progressive ideas, and cultural activity. In contrast, the Sung Dynasty (960–1279) was characterized by economic changes, growth in commerce and trade, and technological innovations. The leaders of the Ming Dynasty (1368–1644) remained focused on agriculture.

In Japan, the Kamakura period (1192–1333) saw the beginning of military rule; the Samurai replaced

nobles as rulers of Japan. During the Muromachi period (1338–1573), the focus was on the military, but with the added influence of Zen Buddhism, Samurai and court society, and artistic traditions. The Edo period (1603–1868) saw Japan unified under a military that maintained the peace for more than two hundred years.

Meanwhile in India, the Gupta Dynasty arose in the fourth century, ushering in India's "Golden Age." A second Golden Age can be claimed for the Mughal Period of the mid-1500s, when the Great Babur (sometimes written as Babar) brought Turkish and Iranian culture to India. Almost thirty years after Babur's death, Akbar the Great took the throne. He was credited with unifying the empire.

The great rulers of Cambodia were the Khmer kings. Revered as demigods, they exercised absolute power. For six hundred years at their capitol at Angkor, they maintained an innovative irrigation infrastructure. This system enabled the Khmer to grow many crops each year, leading to a strong economy.

The West Looks East

No one knows when Europeans first reached the Far East. However it was not until Vasco da Gama pioneered the first all-water route between Europe and Asia (1498) that the East became accessible to the West.

During the eighteenth century, the British began to import opium, a drug, into China despite Chinese laws prohibiting it. In 1838, the Chinese government seized and destroyed thousands of chests of British opium, launching the Opium War. The Chinese suffered a humiliating loss, and China was forced to cede the island of Hong Kong.

England was not the only country with colonial intentions in Asia. France asserted control over much of Indochina in the late nineteenth century—a region that consisted of Laos, Cambodia, and present-day Vietnam. As World War II ended, the French announced a plan that would allow for more independence among the colonies. The plan was accepted by Cambodia and Laos, but Vietnamese nationalists demanded total independence. The war between Vietnam and France lasted nearly a decade, ending with the French defeat at Dien Bien Phu.

The Gate of Ishtar at the entrance to Ancient Babylon. This structure was dedicated by King Nebuchadnezzar II in the 600s B.C.

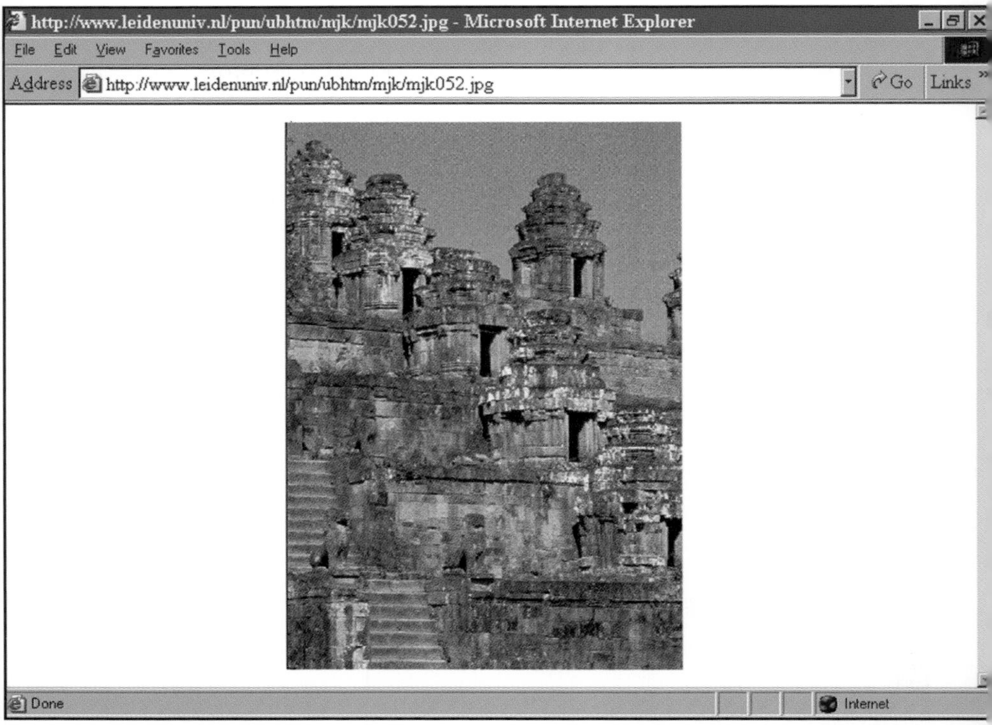

http://www.leidenuniv.nl/pun/ubhtm/mjk/mjk052.jpg - Microsoft Internet Explorer

File Edit View Favorites Tools Help

Address http://www.leidenuniv.nl/pun/ubhtm/mjk/mjk052.jpg Go Links

Done Internet

The State Temple in Angkor, Cambodia, was built during the reign of the Khmer kings.

The beginning of the Sino-Japanese War in 1894 touched off a frenzy of Japanese imperialism. During the next five decades, Japan invaded and occupied Korea, Manchuria, China, and Indochina. The end began in 1941 when the Japanese bombed Hawaii's Pearl Harbor during World War II. In 1945, the war ended in Asia when the United States dropped atomic bombs on Hiroshima and Nagasaki, Japan.

Modern History

The Middle East has been in a constant state of war since the creation of a Jewish national home in Palestine in

1923. Tensions between Arabs and Jews rose even higher when the Jewish national home gained nation status as the State of Israel in 1948. While various groups and nations have signed peace treaties with Israel over the years, others have remained at war. They challenge the legitimacy of the state of Israel and accuse Israelis of illegally occupying Arab land.

Both Korea and Vietnam became hot spots during the Cold War between the United States and the Soviet Union. Communism spread from the Soviet Union to Indochina and the Korean Peninsula, and the United States feared that the Soviets would infiltrate all of Southeast Asia. Ultimately, United States fears of communism dissolved with the fall of the Soviet Union in the 1990s.

Tiananmen Square is located in Beijing, China. The portrait in the background is of former Chinese leader Mao Tse-tung. General Mao was the leader of China's Communist party and the People's Republic of China.

The Tokyo Tower in Japan was completed in 1958 as a symbol of the nation's rise to one of the world's strongest economies.

In China, the twentieth century saw the end of the traditional succession of dynasties. The People's Republic of China was established in 1949 with Mao Tse-tung as the new republic's leader. At that time, China was concerned with economic stability while establishing a Socialist state. The cultural revolution (1966–76) was Mao's misguided attempt to avoid a Soviet-style Socialist bureaucracy. The revolution resulted in the persecution of Chinese intellectuals and educators as well as a dramatic drop in industrial productivity.

After World War II and the Korean War, Japan's economy flourished. The economic growth resulted in a dramatic increase in the standard of living. The Japanese, however, became heavily dependent on foreign oil sources. The 1973 oil crisis stunned their economy, and, in response, Japanese industry shifted to a focus on high technology. The high-tech explosion spread to other parts of Asia, notably South Korea and Taiwan, and remains a primary part of Asian industry into the twenty-first century.

The population of Asia is exploding, despite efforts to control birthrates. Related public health concerns include poverty, malnutrition, and disease. AIDS, though slow to start in Asia, now has a foothold. World Health officials fear it could spread rapidly.

Nuclear tension has become a major concern throughout much of Asia, and it is clear that it will be a focus of international diplomacy for years to come. Currently, Pakistan and India—both nuclear powers—are engaged in an on-again, off-again quarrel. They argue over a portion of land called the Punjab that both countries claim. Wars were fought over concerns Iraq had nuclear capabilities. North Korea also claims to have nuclear weapons.

A Promising Future

As we look to the future of Asia, we should expect to see amazing engineering feats. China's Three Gorges Dam, a mile and a half wide and more than six hundred feet tall, is the biggest construction project since the Great Wall. In Japan, look for the Akashi-Kaikyo Bridge linking Kobe with Awaji Island. With a main span of 6,528 feet, it is the world's longest suspension bridge. In addition, one cannot ignore Malaysia's Petronas Towers. The world's tallest buildings at 1,483 feet, they will continue to be a symbol of how Asia and its people have aspired to new heights for years to come.

Chapter Notes

Chapter 1. World's Largest Continent

1. Borgna Bruner, editor in chief, *Time Almanac 2003* (Boston: Information Please, 2002).

2. Paul Thomas Welty, *The Asians: Their Heritage and Their Destiny* (Philadelphia: J. B. Lippincott Co., 1976), p. 21.

Chapter 3. Animal and Plant Life

1. World Wildlife Fund, "Endangered Species: Tigers," n.d., <http://www.worldwildlife.org/tigers/> (June 28, 2003).

2. World Wildlife Fund, "Endangered Species: Pandas," n.d., <http://www.worldwildlife.org/species/species.cfm?section id=95&newspaperid=21> (June 28, 2003).

3. World Wildlife Fund, "Endangered Species: Elephants," n.d., <http://www.worldwildlife.org/species/species.cfm?section id=26&newspaperid=21> (June 28, 2003).

Chapter 4. People and Culture

1. Tad Szulc, "Abraham: Journey of Faith," *National Geographic*, December 2001, p. 96.

2. PageWise, "Confucius biography and teachings," 2001, <http://allsands.com/History/People/confuciusbiogra_ryh_gn .htm> (June 28, 2003).

3. The Government of Tibet in Exile, "His Holiness the Dalai Lama's Nobel Prize acceptance speech," September 9, 1997, <http://www.tibet.com/DL/nobelaccept.html> (June 28, 2003).

Chapter 5. Economy

1. Paul Thomas Welty, *The Asians: Their Heritage and Their Destiny* (Philadelphia: J.B. Lippincott Co., 1976), p. 30.

Further Reading

Bramwell, Martyn. *Southern and Eastern Asia.* Minneapolis, Minn.: Lerner Publishing Group, 2000.

Brazil, Mark. *Wild Asia: Spirit of a Continent.* Gretna, La.: Pelican Publishing Co., 2000.

Cartlidge, Cherese and Charles Clark. *The Central Asia States.* Farmington Hills, Mich.: Gale Group, 2001.

Lamber, David. *Asia.* Austin, Tex.: Raintree Publishers, 1997.

Major, John S. and Betty J. Belanus. *Caravan to America: Living Arts of the Silk Road.* Chicago: Cricket Books, 2002.

Porter, Malcolm and Keith Lye. *Asia.* Austin, Tex.: Raintree Steck-Vaughn, 2002.

Rutsala, David. *The Sea Route to Asia.* Broomall, Penn.: Mason Crest Publishers, 2002.

Sammis, Fran. *Asia.* New York: Benchmark Books, 1999.

Seabrooke, Kevin, ed. *The World Almanac for Kids.* New York: World Almanac Books, 2002.

Stearns, Peter N., ed. *The Encyclopedia of World History.* New York: Houghton Mifflin, Co., 2001.

Viesti, Joe, and Diane Hall. C*elebrate in South Asia.* New York: Lothrop, Lee & Shepard Books, 1996.

——— . *Celebrate in Southeast Asia!* New York: Lothrop, Lee & Shepard Books, 1996.

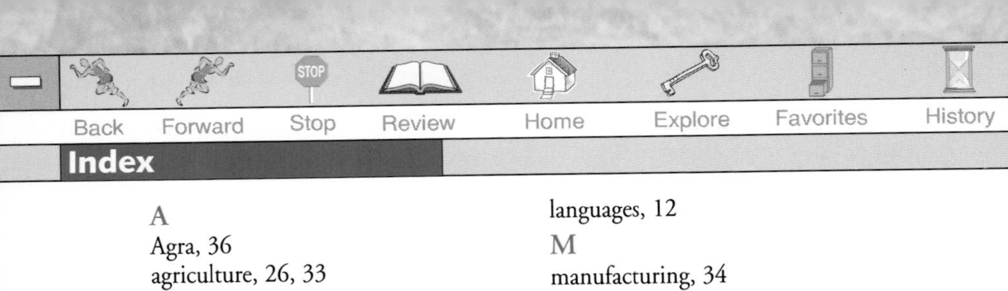
STOP
Back
Forward
Stop
Review
Home
Explore
Favorites
History

Index